That's My Dog
PUGS

by Wendy Hinote Lanier

FOCUS READERS

www.focusreaders.com

Copyright © 2018 by Focus Readers, Lake Elmo, MN 55042. All rights reserved. No part of this book may be reproduced or utilized in any form or by any means without written permission from the publisher.

Focus Readers is distributed by North Star Editions: sales@northstareditions.com | 888-417-0195

Produced for Focus Readers by Red Line Editorial.

Photographs ©: LexiTheMonster/iStockphoto, cover, 1; GCShutter/iStockphoto, 4–5; Ezzolo/Shutterstock Images, 6; India Picture/Shutterstock Images, 8–9; Anton Ivanov/Shutterstock Images, 10; ponpimonsa_bibi/Shutterstock Images, 12; gp88/Shutterstock Images, 14–15; Nataliya Kuznetsova/Shutterstock Images, 16; Olena Savytska/Shutterstock Images, 18; Ken McKay/ITV/REX/Shutterstock, 20–21; WildStrawberry/Shutterstock Images, 22–23, 29; Chernenko Maria/Shutterstock Images, 24; Sjale/iStockphoto, 26

ISBN
978-1-63517-543-1 (hardcover)
978-1-63517-615-5 (paperback)
978-1-63517-759-6 (ebook pdf)
978-1-63517-687-2 (hosted ebook)

Library of Congress Control Number: 2017948136

Printed in the United States of America
Mankato, MN
November, 2017

About the Author

Wendy Hinote Lanier is a native Texan and former elementary science teacher who writes and speaks for children and adults on a variety of topics. She is the author of more than 25 books for children and young adults. Some of her favorite people are dogs.

TABLE OF CONTENTS

CHAPTER 1
Meet the Pug 5

CHAPTER 2
Pugs in the Past 9

CHAPTER 3
The Perfect Pug 15

THAT'S AMAZING!
Doug the Pug 20

CHAPTER 4
Pug Pampering 23

Focus on Pugs • 28
Glossary • 30
To Learn More • 31
Index • 32

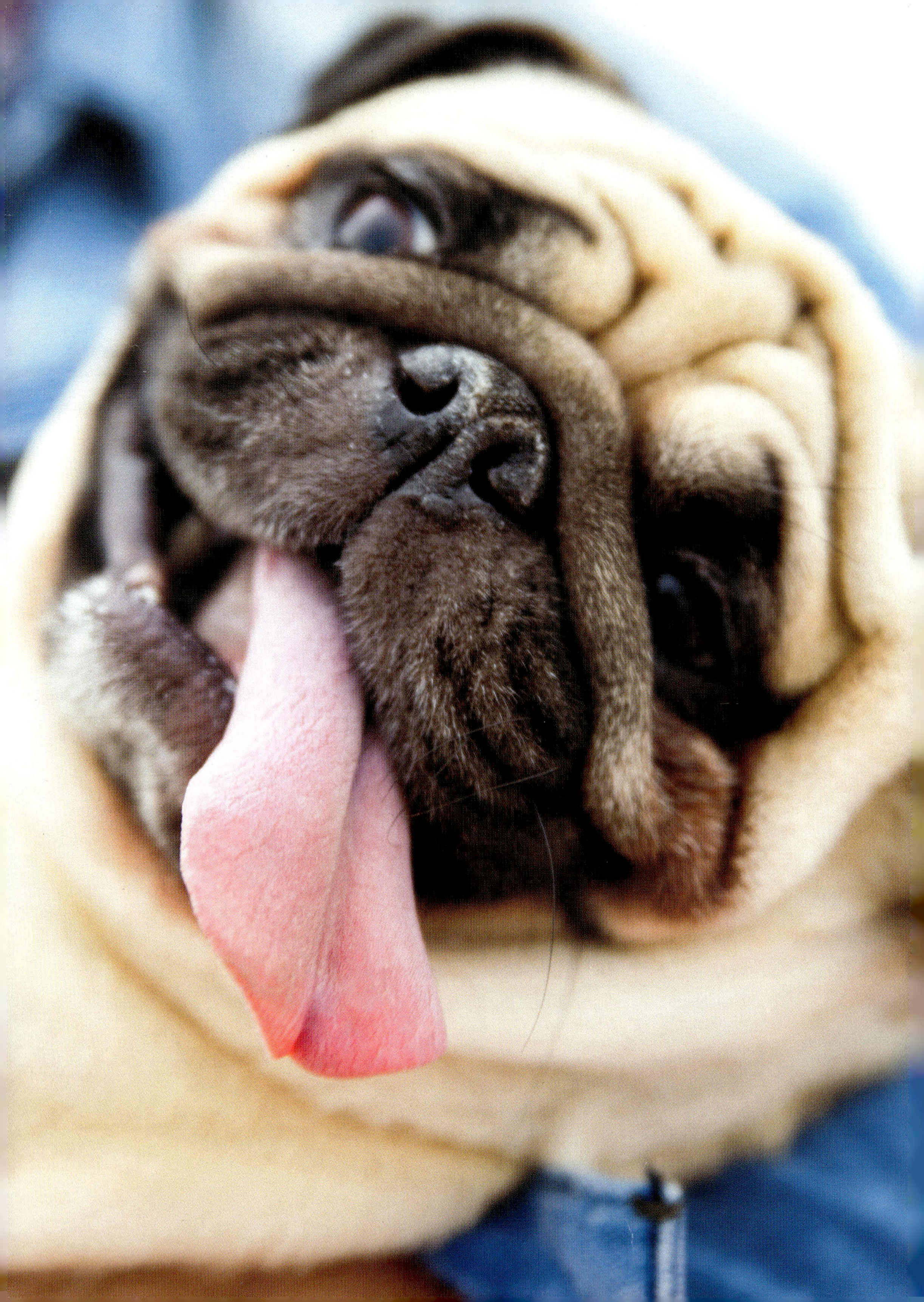

CHAPTER 1

MEET THE PUG

Pugs have big personalities. But they come in small packages. They are little dogs with big hearts.

Pugs are funny and playful. Some people call them the clowns of the dog world. Pugs are curious.

> **Pugs love being around their owners.**

> **Some owners enjoy dressing their pugs in silly costumes.**

Sometimes this gets them into trouble. Most of all, pugs are social dogs. They love being around other dogs, people, and children. This makes them great **companion** dogs.

Pugs are faithful to their friends and owners. They love to be hugged and held. And they are great dogs for families with kids.

FUN FACT

A pug won top honors at an important **dog show** in 1981. It was the first time a pug received this award.

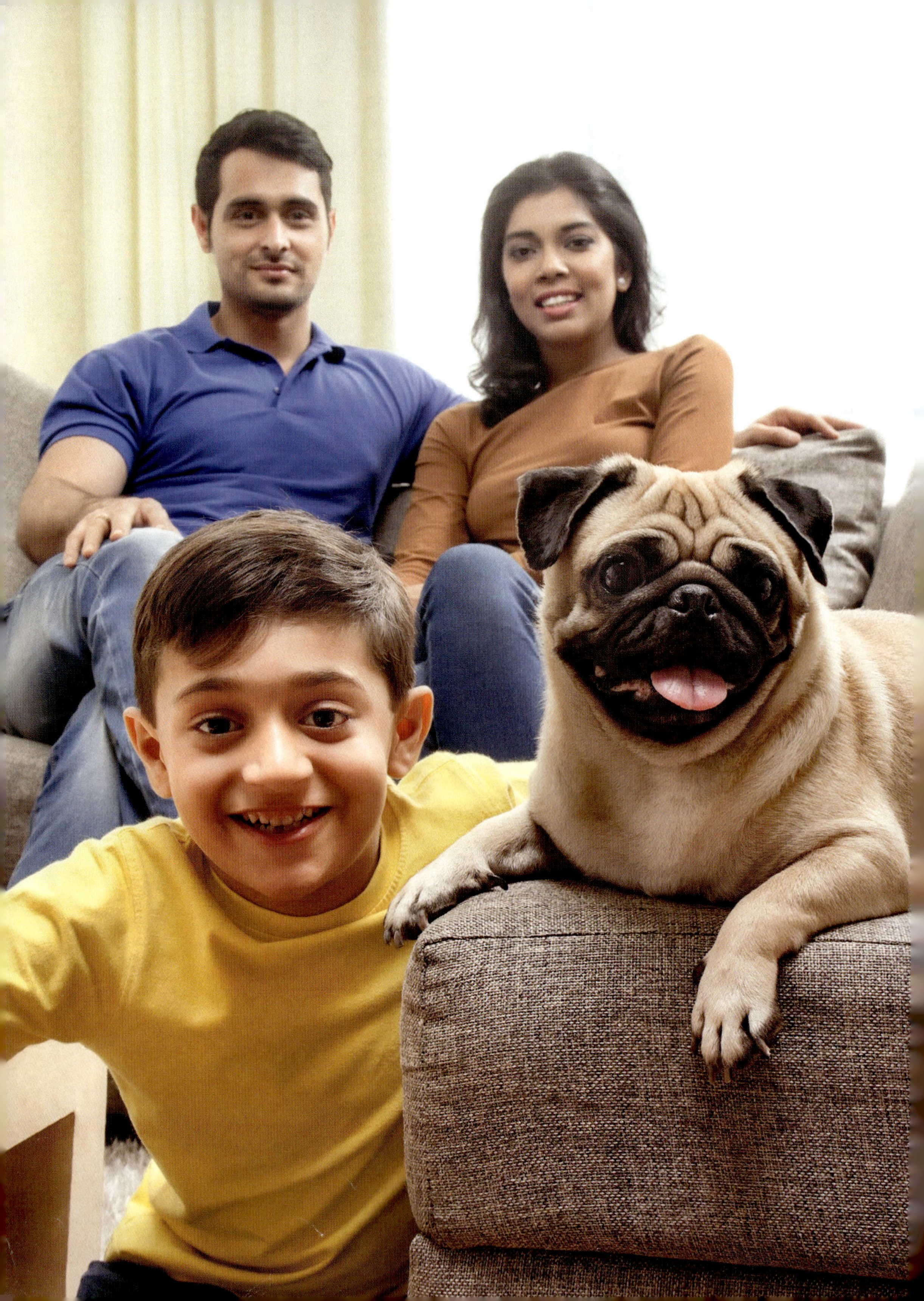

CHAPTER 2

PUGS IN THE PAST

Pugs are one of the oldest dog **breeds**. They originated in China more than 2,000 years ago. Pugs are related to the Pekingese. That is a small, long-haired breed. It has short legs and a flat nose.

▷ **Today, pugs are popular all over the world.**

▷ **Many ancient Chinese monasteries still stand today.**

The first pugs were pets for **monks**. These monks lived in the mountains. They spent their lives in

monasteries. The pugs kept them company there.

Pugs were also pets for Chinese **emperors**. The emperors gave pugs as gifts to people in other countries. Over time, pugs became common in Japan and Europe. Pugs were a favorite of royalty there, too.

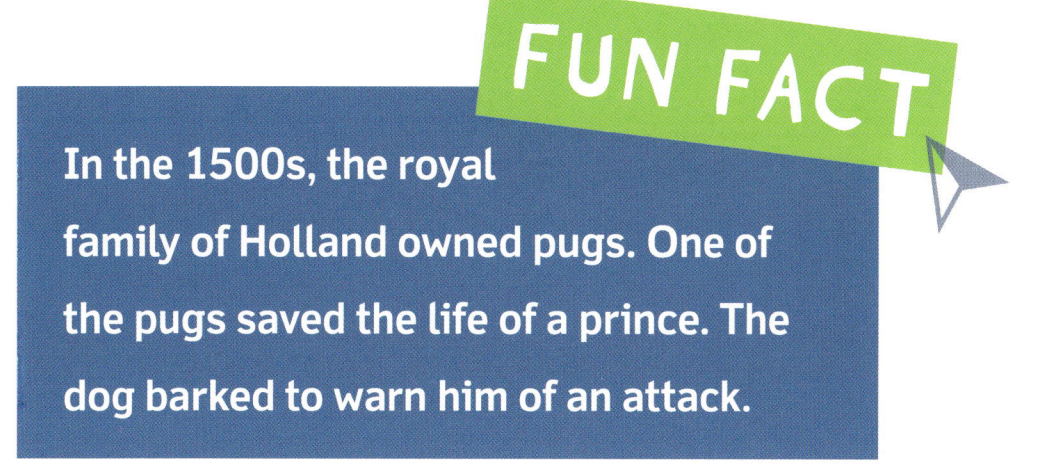

FUN FACT

In the 1500s, the royal family of Holland owned pugs. One of the pugs saved the life of a prince. The dog barked to warn him of an attack.

Today's pugs have flatter faces than early pugs.

Pugs arrived in the United States in the 1800s. The American Kennel Club (AKC) accepted pugs as a breed in 1885. The AKC is a group that keeps track of different dog breeds. Pugs belong to the AKC Toy Group. This is a group of the smallest dog breeds.

FUN FACT

England's Queen Victoria had several pugs. She made pugs popular in England in the 1800s.

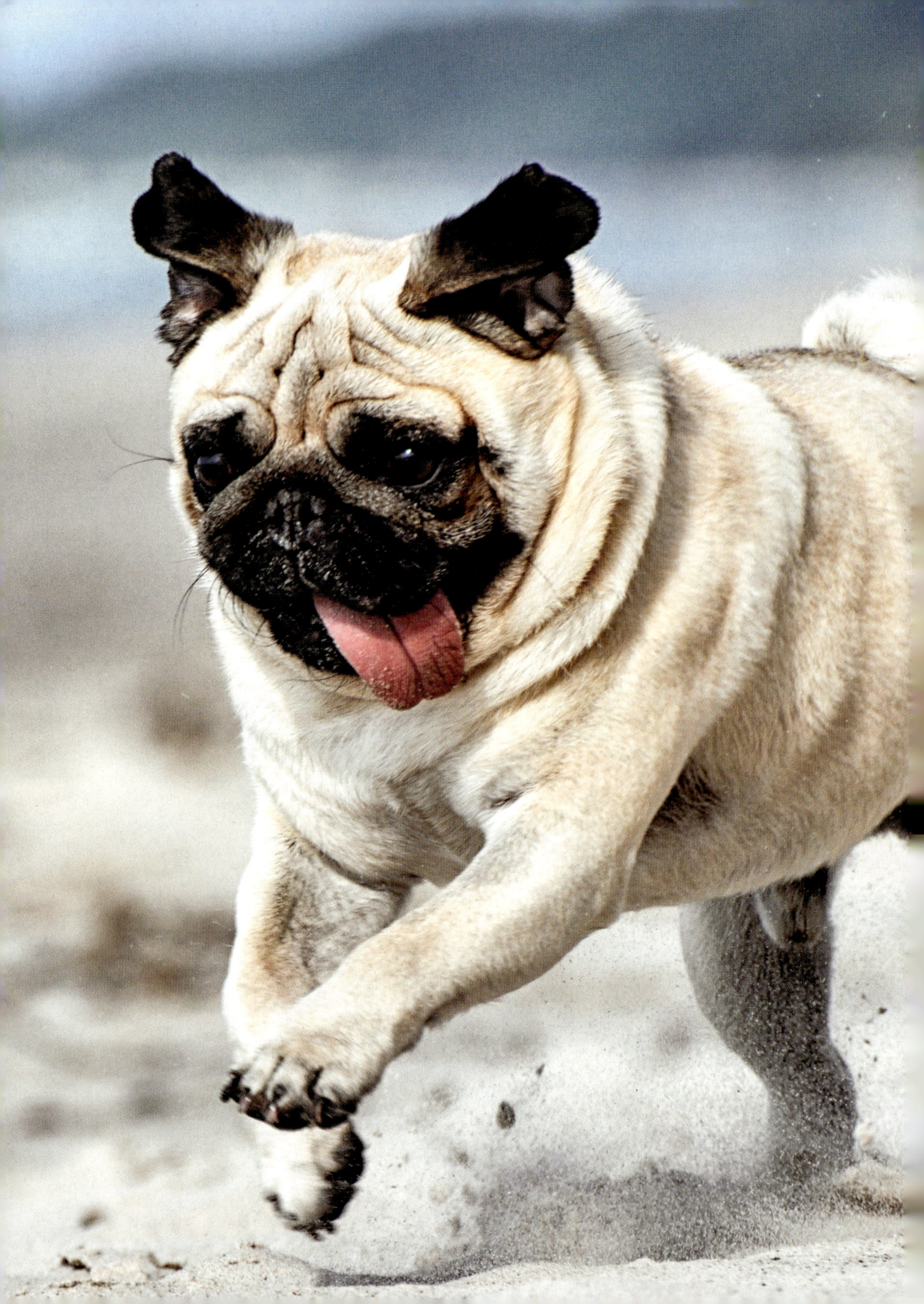

CHAPTER 3

THE PERFECT PUG

Pugs are easy to spot in a crowd. They are small, square-shaped dogs with round heads. They have flat, wrinkled faces. The fur across a pug's nose and mouth is black. It looks like a black mask.

> Sometimes a pug's tongue sticks out when it runs.

> **It takes pug puppies about a year to reach their full height.**

A pug's coat is short and smooth.

The dog's tail curls over its back.

Most pugs come in two colors. They

are often **fawn** or black. But pugs come in other colors, too. Some are silver, and others are light orange.

Adult pugs weigh approximately 16 pounds (7.3 kg). Pugs are approximately 12 inches (30 cm) tall when they are full grown.

FUN FACT

Pugs fit in well with both young and old families. They are active and playful with young children. But they can be calm companions to the elderly.

Sometimes pugs look like they are smiling.

Pugs have large, round eyes. Their small ears are velvety. Pugs have expressive faces. They often tip their heads to one side when someone is speaking. They seem to pay attention to every word.

Pugs are not **yappy** dogs. Instead, their bark is low-pitched and gruff. Pugs are also known for snorting and snoring. These noises are caused by the pug's flat face.

FUN FACT

Pugs are the largest dog breed in the AKC's Toy Group.

THAT'S AMAZING!

DOUG THE PUG

Dog lover Leslie Mosier had a pug named Doug. When Doug was a puppy, Leslie dressed Doug in funny costumes. Then she took pictures.

Leslie posted the pictures of Doug on her **social media** accounts. People began to take notice. Soon, Doug had millions of fans.

Doug the Pug became the most popular pug on the web. Doug starred in his own videos. Leslie even created calendars with pictures of Doug. She wrote a book about him, too. People couldn't get enough of this adorable pug.

Doug got to travel and be on television with his owner, Leslie.

21

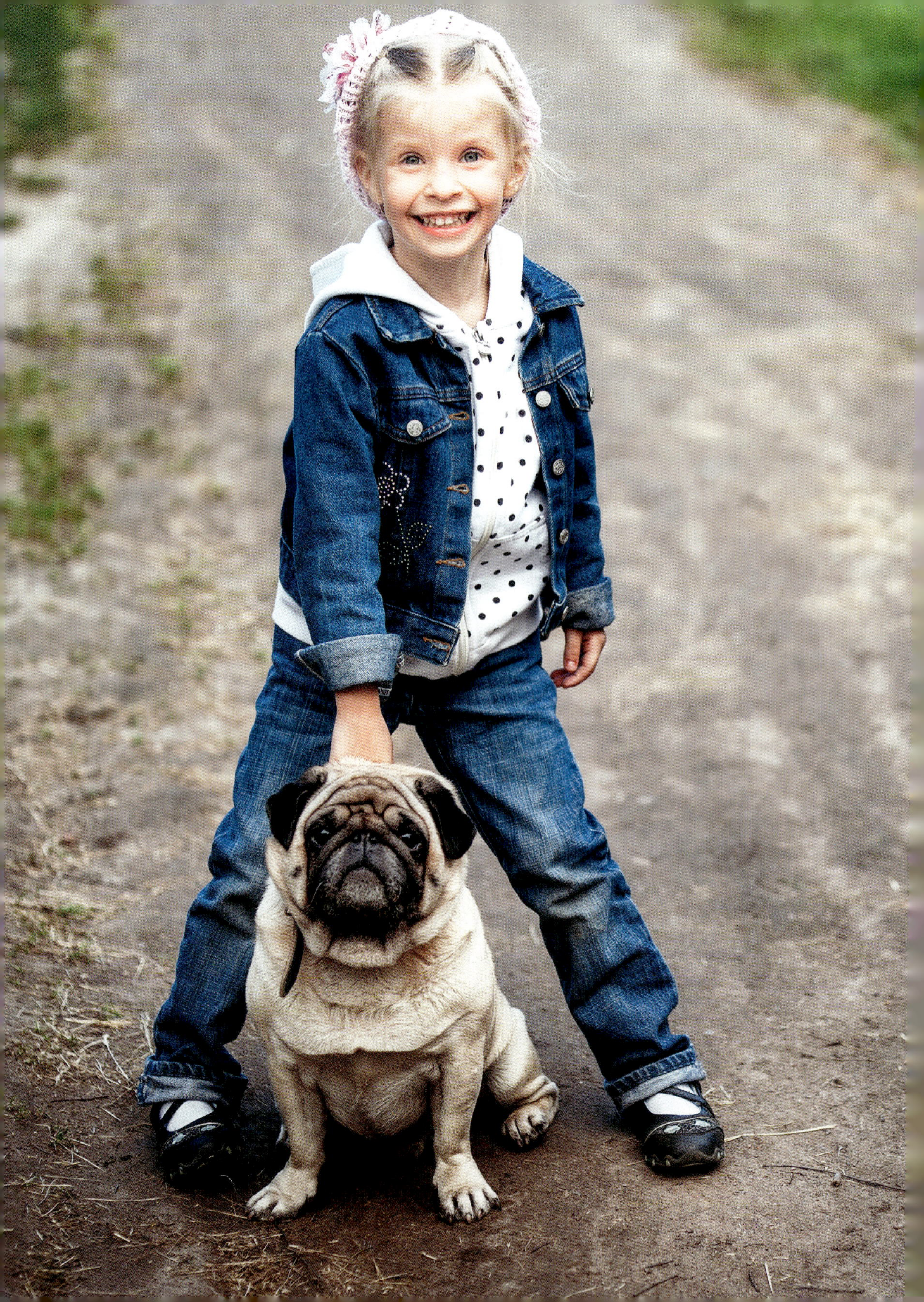

CHAPTER 4

PUG PAMPERING

Pugs have the same basic needs as other dogs. But they also have specific needs. For example, pugs often have breathing problems. This happens because pugs have short noses and flat faces.

Pugs are friendly to other pets and children.

▷ **A short walk is all pugs need to use up their energy.**

Pugs also catch colds easily. These dogs should not get too hot or too cold. It is best

24

to keep them inside at a comfortable temperature.

Pugs are good apartment dogs. They do not need a lot of exercise. A short daily walk is just right. But be sure to use a harness. Pulling on a leash attached to a collar can make it hard for a pug to breathe.

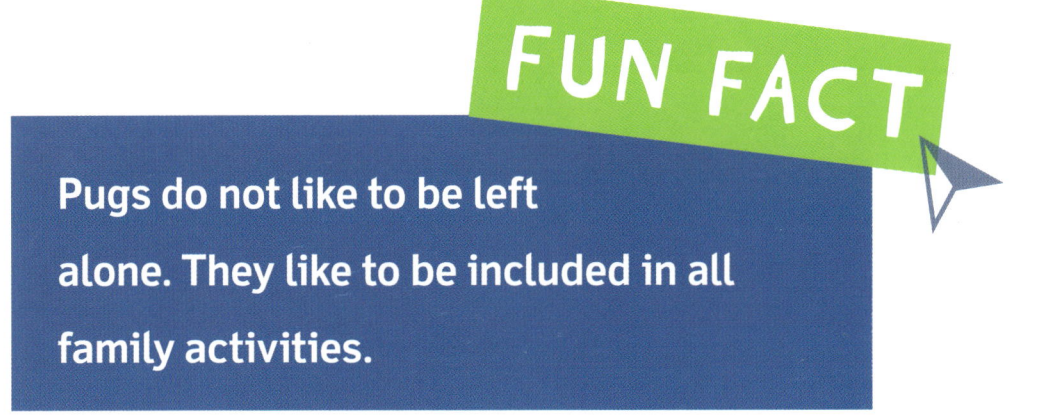

FUN FACT

Pugs do not like to be left alone. They like to be included in all family activities.

▶ **Treats can be helpful when training a pug.**

Pugs are known for **shedding**. They need a good brushing at least once a week. The wrinkles on their face should be cleaned often.

Pugs can be stubborn. This means house-training a pug can take patience. Luckily, a pug will do anything for food. Just be careful not to feed the pug too much.

Training can be a lot of work. But a pug's personality makes it a fun pet for many owners.

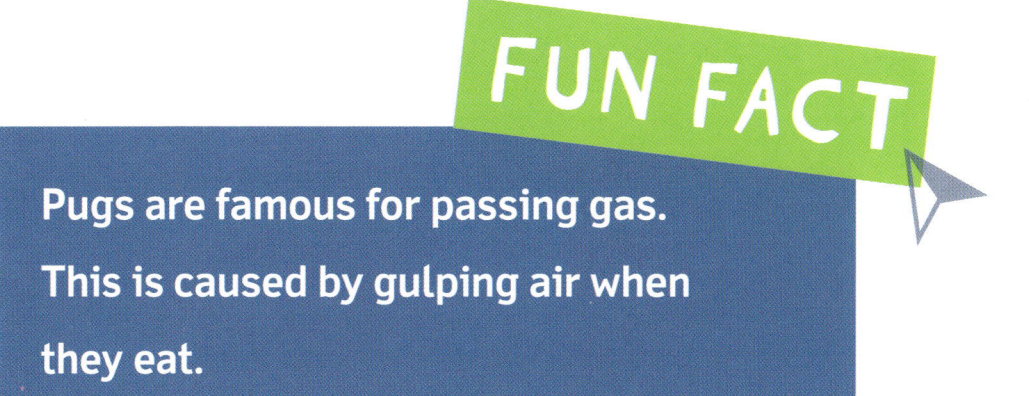

FUN FACT

Pugs are famous for passing gas. This is caused by gulping air when they eat.

FOCUS ON
PUGS

Write your answers on a separate piece of paper.

1. Write a letter to a friend describing the main ideas of Chapter 4.

2. Would you like to own a pug? Why or why not?

3. Where did pugs first come from?
- **A.** Holland
- **B.** China
- **C.** the United States

4. How might a pug react to being left alone?
- **A.** It would be lazy.
- **B.** It would be happy.
- **C.** It would be lonely.

5. What does **originated** mean in this book?

*Pugs are one of the oldest dog breeds. They **originated** in China more than 2,000 years ago.*

　　A. got older
　　B. started
　　C. grew taller

6. What does **expressive** mean in this book?

*Pugs have **expressive** faces. They often tip their heads to one side when someone is speaking. They seem to pay attention to every word.*

　　A. showing no emotion
　　B. appearing to be in pain
　　C. showing thoughts and feelings

Answer key on page 32.

GLOSSARY

breeds
Groups of animals that share the same looks and features.

companion
A person or animal who spends a lot of time with another.

dog show
A competition where different dogs are judged based on the standard for their breed.

emperors
People who rule over a country or empire.

fawn
A tan or light-brown color.

monasteries
Places where monks work and live, similar to a church.

monks
People who belong to a religious group.

shedding
Releasing dead hair.

social media
Forms of communication that allow people to connect on the internet.

yappy
Having frequent, high-pitched barks.

TO LEARN MORE

BOOKS

Gagne, Tammy. *Chihuahuas, Pomeranians, and Other Toy Dogs*. North Mankato, MN: Capstone Press, 2017.

Mosier, Leslie. *Doug the Pug: King of Pop Culture*. New York: Saint Martin's Griffin, 2016.

Newman, Aline Alexander, and Gary Weitzman. *How to Speak Dog: A Guide to Decoding Dog Language*. Washington, DC: National Geographic, 2013.

NOTE TO EDUCATORS

Visit **www.focusreaders.com** to find lesson plans, activities, links, and other resources related to this title.

INDEX

A
American Kennel Club (AKC), 13

B
breathing, 23

C
China, 9–11
coat, 16–17

D
dog shows, 7
Doug the Pug, 20

E
England, 13
Europe, 11
exercise, 25

F
faces, 15, 18–19, 23, 26
families, 7, 17, 25

H
height, 17
Holland, 11

J
Japan, 11

M
Mosier, Leslie, 20

P
Pekingese, 9

S
shedding, 26

T
Toy Group, 13, 19
training, 27

W
weight, 17
wrinkles, 15, 26

Answer Key: 1. Answers will vary; 2. Answers will vary; 3. B; 4. C; 5. B; 6. C